# THE BOOK OF DOOF
## HOW TO FIND AN ARCH NEMESIS AND OTHER EVIL ADVICE

By Scott Peterson

Based on the series created by Dan Povenmire & Jeff "Swampy" Marsh

DISNEY PRESS
New York • Los Angeles

"Dr. Heinz Doofenshmirtz's Tales of Drusselstein" comic insert one—Writer: Scott Peterson, Pencils: Eric Jones, Inks: Mike DeCarlo, Colors: Garry Black, Letters: Michael Stewart

"The Comic Hijinks of Norm and Doof" comic insert one— Writer: Scott Peterson, Pencils, Inks, Colors, & Letters: John Green

"Night of the Goozim" comic insert one—Writer: Scott Peterson, Pencils: Scott Neely, Inks: Mike DeCarlo, Colors: Emily Kanalz, Letters: Michael Stewart

"Dr. Heinz Doofenshmirtz's Tales of Drusselstein" comic insert two—Writer: Scott Peterson, Pencils & Inks: Min Sung Ku, Colors: Garry Black, Letters: Michael Stewart

"Agent in Training" comic insert two—Writer: Scott Peterson, Pencils: Fabricio Grellet & Magic Eye Studios, Inks: Mike DeCarlo, Colors: Wes Dzioba, Letters: Michael Stewart

"The Substitute" comic insert two—Writer: Scott Peterson, Pencils: John Green, Inks: Mike DeCarlo, Colors: Wes Dzioba, Letters: Michael Stewart

"The Comic Hijinks of Norm and Doof" comic insert two— Writer: Scott Peterson, Pencils & Inks: Tom Neely, Colors: Emily Kanalz, Letters: Michael Stewart

"Perry the . . . Octopus?" comic insert two—Writer: Scott Peterson, Pencils & Inks: Eric Jones, Colors: Wes Dzioba, Letters: Michael Stewart

Printed in the United States of America

First Edition

10 9 8 7 6 5 4 3 2 1

G475-5664-5-13335

ISBN 978-1-4231-7928-3

Library of Congress Control Number: 2013937580

For more Disney Press fun, visit www.disneybooks.com

Visit DisneyChannel.com

SUSTAINABLE FORESTRY INITIATIVE    Certified Sourcing
www.sfiprogram.org
SFI-00993

THIS LABEL APPLIES TO TEXT STOCK

# TABLE OF CONTENTS

**Foreword** . . . . . . . . . . . . . . . . . . . . . . . . . . . . . . . . 5

**Chapter 1:** All About Doof! . . . . . . . . . . . . . . . . 7

**Chapter 2:** A History of Evil . . . . . . . . . . . . . . .21

**Chapter 3:** Evil from A to Z . . . . . . . . . . . . . . . . 41

**Chapter 4:** Evil and You . . . . . . . . . . . . . . . . . . .51

**Chapter 5:** Refining Your Villainous Persona . . . . . . . 81

**Chapter 6:** The One Secret to Instant Evil Success . . . . 99

**Chapter 7:** My Arch Nemesis . . . . . . . . . . . . . . . 101

**Chapter 8:** Your Arch Nemesis . . . . . . . . . . . . . . 115

**Chapter 9:** -Inators and You . . . . . . . . . . . . . . . . 129

**Conclusion** . . . . . . . . . . . . . . . . . . . . . . . . . . 144

I KNOW YOU WANT TO STAMPEDE STRAIGHT TO CHAPTER 6 AND INSTANT EVIL SUCCESS, BUT HOLD YOUR HORSES, KEMOSABE. YOU'RE NOT READY FOR IT. SERIOUSLY. I'M WARNING YOU.

What goes on the back of the table of contents? I have no idea. I mean, you have to put *something* there because you can't start the book on an *even* page. No one will take you seriously.

Most people skip right over the dedication and the introduction anyway, and the back side of the contents page is even less important than that, so it's really just wasted space.

But as long as I've got this whole blank canvas in front of me, a whole page to defile, I figured I'd do one of my world-famous artistic renderings. And by "world-famous" I mean "Norm likes them." And by "artistic renderings" I mean "poorly drawn doodles."

# FOREWORD

If you have purchased this book I can only assume
that your life is so misguided that you are turning to me,
Dr. Heinz Doofenshmirtz, for advice. You believe that a man
who has spent most of his adult life failing to take over the
Tri-State Area possesses the knowledge you seek to improve
your life. You were willing to plunk down your hard-earned
cash to read the ramblings of a man who gets thwarted by
an animal one-third his size day after day after day.

Well, you've come to the right place.

In this book that you hold in your hands (I assume it's in your hands—if it's not, I don't want to know), I have distilled all of my hard-won life experience into easy-to-understand chapters that will help you to become the evil person you were meant to be. Learning from my voluminous mistakes, you will discover the villainy within you, find your own arch nemesis, and, hopefully, defeat that nemesis in your ill-fated bid for ultimate power.

So read on, fellow ne'er-do-well, and stay evil!

# CHAPTER 1:
# ALL ABOUT DOOF!

In order to properly understand where I'm "coming from" (to use a phrase the kids are "hip" to), you need to know where I've been, who I am now, where I'm going, and what kind of toilet paper I prefer. In other words, you need to know ME!

I'm Dr. Heinz Doofenshmirtz, born in the unforgiving mountains of Gimmelshtump and settled in the mean streets of Danville, high atop the irregularly shaped building known as Doofenshmirtz Evil Incorporated. While people on the street may mistake me for a pharmacist (if they notice me at all), I am in fact an evil scientist and reasonably proud member of L.O.V.E.M.U.F.F.I.N., the League of Villains, Evil, Monsters, something or other. It takes way too long to write. Who needs such a long, rambly acronym anyway?

I strive each and every day to defeat my nemesis, Perry the Platypus, and take over the Tri-State Area, often through the use of a twisted scheme and a poorly designed –inator . . . that inevitably self-destructs.

But that only scratches the surface of all that is Heinz.

# TOP TEN MOST EVIL THINGS ABOUT HEINZ DOOFENSHMIRTZ!

1. I take sugar packets from restaurants. As many as my pockets can hold.

2. When I eat chips at a party, I always double dip.

3. Sometimes when Perry is busy, I thwart Peter the Panda behind his back.

4. I set mousetraps with no cheese in them. Why should the mice get my perfectly good cheese?

5. I try incessantly to take over the Tri-State Area. But you knew that, right?

6. I've been up in the tower three times. (Whoops! That's from the Ten Most Eiffel Things About Heinz Doofenshmirtz.)

7. I purposely call people right at dinnertime. Annoy-ing!

8. Okay, this isn't really evil, but I hide when the Fireside Girls come over to sell cupcakes.

9. I write letters to Santa from Roger asking for things he already has.

10. I spend all day, every day, working as an evil scientist. It's right there in my title: EVIL!

# FROM THE MOUTH OF HEINZ

You know that old saying "Words speak louder than actions!" Or maybe it's the other way around, I don't know. But clearly when you say things, it has something to do with what you are thinking, right? So to better understand the enigma of me, take a look at these words of wisdom from yours truly.

ALL MY LIFE I'VE BEEN A ZERO, BUT NOW I'LL BE *TWICE* THAT!

PERRY THE PLATYPUS, WHAT AN UNEXPECTED SURPRISE. AND BY UNEXPECTED, I REALLY MEAN UNEXPECTED. WHAT ARE YOU DOING HERE? THIS IS MY WEEK OFF.

THE MOLTEN LAVA AT THE EARTH'S CORE COMPLETELY SLIPPED MY MIND.

THAT SOUNDED LIKE SCREAMING CHILDREN. BUT IT'S NOT MY BIRTHDAY.

IF I HAD A NICKEL FOR EVERY TIME I'VE BEEN DOOMED BY A PUPPET, I WOULD HAVE TWO NICKELS. THAT'S NOT A LOT, BUT IT'S FUNNY THAT IT HAPPENED TWICE.

# THE SECRET TO MY EVIL SUCCESS

One of the most important things I can pass on to you is the secret to my evil success. Now some people may debate how successful I've actually been since I haven't *technically* succeeded at taking over the Tri-State Area . . . yet.

But even if I haven't had much evil success, I have been successful at *being* evil. It's a fine line, but one that I cling to for my own self-esteem.

So what is the secret to my success at being evil? Painful backstories. My early life in Gimmelshtump was hard (my parents didn't even show up for my birth!) and turned me from an innocent child into the evil man I am today.

So if you can take one piece of advice from this book, remember to have a horrible childhood. Good luck!

# THE DOOFENSHMIRTZ WAY: HOW TO FIGHT A PLANT

Okay, clearly by now you're getting tired of reading about me and my life and you want some serious, hands-on, "how-to" information to improve your evil standing. Well, get ready to learn big time.

1. **Don't underestimate your opponent.**
   I know what you're thinking. "A plant can't move. This is gonna be easy!" That's your first mistake.

2. **Don't get smug.**
   I'm telling you, Planty the Potted Plant is a force to be reckoned with. He's no Perry the Platypus, but this ferny foe has got some moves.

3. **Use a blanket.**
   Throw a blanket over it and wait. With no sun or water, your planty nemesis will wilt within days . . . or possibly weeks. I hope you bring this book to read while you wait.

# DOOF TRIVIA

Okay, Smarty McSmartypants, let's see how much you really know about me!

## 1) Where did I grow up as a child?

A) Gimmelshtump

B) Drusselstein

C) A distressed Eastern European country

D) All of the above

## 2) Which of these jobs and occupations have I NOT tried?

A) Bratwurst salesman

B) Pizza delivery boy

C) Artist

D) Poet

E) Magician

F) Dry cleaner

**3) What color are my eyes?**

    A) Brown like dirt

    B) Teal like my enemy, Perry the Platypus

    C) Green like something green

    D) Black like my heart

**4) Why is Vanessa so annoyed with me?**

    No, seriously, I'm asking. Does anyone know? I'd like to know what I did.

**5) What was my first -inator called?**

    A) -Inator

    B) The Disgust-inator

    C) The Stinky Mattress-inator

    D) The Crab Salad-inator

**6) Why did I first build Norm?**

    A) For companionship

    B) For a science fair

    C) As an enemy for Perry

    D) Mardi Gras!

**7) What is my favorite thing to eat?**

A) Figgy pudding

B) Almond brittle

C) Raw asparagus

D) My words

**8) How do I pay for my suite at the top of the Doofenshmirtz Evil Incorporated building?**

A) I own the building. Duh!

B) Okay, not the whole building, but I own the top floor.

C) Alimony from my ex-wife covers the rent.

D) Isn't this getting a little personal? Do I ask you about your financial situation? I don't think so.

## SCORING:

Okay, so count up the number of answers you got right and see how you did.

**1–2 Right:** Sorry, Charlie. You really need to read this book.

**3–4 Right:** Not bad. You know your Doof.

**5–6 Right:** Excellent! You know me better than I know myself.

**7–8 Right:** Okay, now this is just getting creepy. Have you been following me or something

**ANSWERS:**

1) **D**—It was lousy.

2) **F**—Not that I have anything against dry cleaners.

3) **D**—I actually have extraordinarily large pupils.

4) **You tell me.**

5) **A**—I wasn't as creative back then.

6) **C**—The natural enemy of the platypus is man . . . so I built a robot.

7) **B**—Loooove it!

8) **C**—Thank you, Charlene.

# BEHOLD! THE -INATOR!

The key to any successful evil scheme is a powerful -inator. This can be almost any machine or device you create with the word "-inator" stuck on the end. A Sliced-bread-inator. A Rhino-waxing-inator. A Get-me-an-ice-cream-scoop-inator. You get the idea.

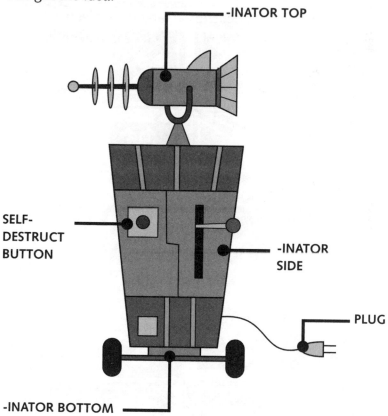

-INATOR TOP

SELF-
DESTRUCT
BUTTON

-INATOR
SIDE

PLUG

-INATOR BOTTOM

The importance of the -inator cannot be overstated. In fact, I should probably devote a whole chapter to them. Hmmm. Okay, forget about this page. Pretend you never saw it.

# DOOF'S FAVORITE RECIPES
## SIMPLE RECIPES FOR THE EVIL SCIENTIST ON THE GO!

They say the way to a man's heart is through his stomach. Clearly, they've never taken even the most basic anatomy class, because the heart and stomach don't connect at all.

But even an evil scientist needs to eat, and maybe you'll gain a little insight into my way of thinking as I reveal a few of Doof's favorite recipes!

## PLATYPUS BURGER

First, catch a platypus. Then carefully cut—KIDDING! Just kidding. Okay, on to the real recipes.

## PEANUT BUTTER AND SARDINE SANDWICH

A Gimmelshtump classic! Take two pieces of mold-free bread and apply peanut butter. (It must be CHUNKY peanut butter. If you have to ask why, it's already too late for you.) Push the sardines into the layers of peanut butter, bring the bread together, and voilà! Instant heartburn!

# MACARONI AND CHEAP

Unlike the all-too-expensive macaroni and cheese, this recipe saves you money by getting rid of that pricey cheese entirely. Instead take FREE packets of mustard from fast-food restaurants and squirt the contents into your noodles for a tasty dish of Macaroni and Cheap!

# WIRED FOR EVIL

**Finish the Evil Blueprint**

This was destined to be my greatest -inator but I was rudely interrupted by a certain platypus who shall remain nameless . . . Perry the Platypus. Anyway, I would greatly appreciate it if you could finish it for me by connecting the final wires, A to A, B to B, and C to C.

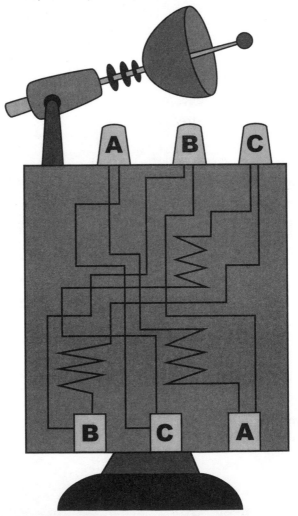

# CHAPTER 2:
# A HISTORY OF EVIL

Well, now that you know all about me, your evil education has begun. But villainy didn't start with me, and there are great examples and colorful stories of evil throughout history.

From the first caveman who rose up and whacked his buddy over the head with a club to take over his Tri-Cave Area, to the industrial-era businessman who created an assembly line to mass-produce evil items for the general populace, mankind has always had an evil streak.

It is important for you to understand the awful steps these men and women took in the past to make evil possible for you today. You may be inspired. You may be amazed. You may be bored . . . that's what history usually does to me. But I'll leave you with the words of the immortal guy whose name I don't remember who said:

"Those who don't know evil history are doomed to repeat it."

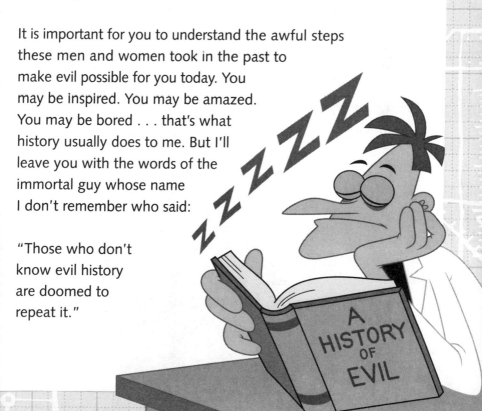

# EVIL WORLD RECORDS

Throughout history, these are the evildoers who did it the longest, the fastest, and the stupidest.

**Longest Evil Monologue:** *2 hours and 48 minutes*
Vilkin Smedgemore reached this milestone in 1983, not realizing that his nemesis had left after the first fifteen minutes.

**Fastest Defeat:** *.2 seconds*
That one's mine. But to be fair, I was a bit under the weather at the time, and Perry the Platypus was in top form, soooo . . . it's still humiliating.

**Longest Evil Name:** *Aloyse Everheart Elizabeth Otto Wolfgang Hypatia Gunther Galen Gary Cooper von Roddenstein*
Known as Rodney to his friends (if he had any), this lengthily named scientist is a member of L.O.V.E.M.U.F.F.I.N. and a big jerk.

## Most Evil Involving a Pet Store: *36 rats*
Lucretia Pinero stole thirty-six rats from a local pet store and let them loose in a cheese store. Wow! Why can't I meet a nice girl like this?

## Most Ridiculous Backstory: *Alien abduction*
Dr. Diminutive once tried to convince his nemesis that he was still emotionally scarred from an abduction by an alien race of whalemingos. How is that scarring? It sounds awesome!

## Farthest Evil Shot-put Throw: *50 feet, 3 inches*
It's not that impressive as a shot-put throw, but as an EVIL shot-put throw, it holds the record. I don't even know the guy's name. I don't need that kind of useless info clogging up my brain.

**Heaviest Trap: *15.2 tons***

This massive cage was designed by Emilio Fitz to capture and hold an elephant agent. Unfortunately, the nemesis assigned to Emilio was a mouse who could walk right through the bars, so . . .

**Most Failures in One Year: *365***

Okay, this one is mine too. But as somebody once said, "You'll never succeed if you don't keep trying." I, on the other hand, never succeed and I DO keep trying, so go figure.

# GREAT EVIL ROLE MODELS

Kids today need someone to look up to, someone to emulate. That's true for evil kids too. Luckily, it's much easier for today's kiddies because they can look up to yours truly, Dr. Heinz Doofenshmirtz. When I was a youth, it was much harder, but a few villainous figures did stand out.

### The Kinderlumper
Ancient Drusselstinian legend tells of this horrible creature that punishes children who don't fall asleep right away. But how is a kid supposed to sleep knowing this nut job is watching him, huh?!

### Victor "Happy Eyes" Filthhaven
This guy started an orphanage right here in the Tri-State Area. Sounds good, right? Then he forced all the orphanage kids to build cheap, defective toys to sell to other kids at a huge profit. What a total jerk. This guy's my hero.

## Señora Spotless

You remember her, right? The lady in those ads for Spotless Whole House Cleaner? What kind of woman cleans her house in a wedding dress? I'll tell you what kind . . . an EVIL one!

## Captain Courage

I know this guy sounds like a superhero or something, but he was just a man with an old bedsheet for a cape who took over half of South America before fleeing into the jungle, never to be seen again. Wait, why is this guy even on the list?

## My Mom

I don't know that she was consciously trying to be an evil role model, but there isn't an evil event that occurs in the world that doesn't remind me of my mother.

# EVIL IN THE OLD WEST

People who talk about "the good old days" certainly aren't thinking about the Wild West. Towns like Tombstone and Deadwood had some of the meanest, dirtiest, ugliest, evilest people in all history. And those were the women!

## Cowboys

They may seem heroic in the old black-and-white Westerns on TV, but these guys rarely bathed, never picked up after their horses, and spit more than modern-day baseball players. Yuck!

## Cattle Rustlers

Same as cowboys, but they also steal Bessie, your prize cow.

### Bandits

These are the guys in the wanted posters with the bandanas over their faces. Why was the bandana invented anyway? The only time I ever see one is covering the face of a bandit. Anyhow, these guys robbed banks, robbed trains, robbed stagecoaches, and, when desperate, they robbed each other.

### Crooked Sheriffs

The sheriff is supposed to guard the pokey (the jail), keep the peace, and chase bandits and ne'er-do-wells out of town, but he's about as helpful as a tumbleweed in an outhouse if he goes bad. He says things like "'Round here, I'm the law" and then takes your gold.

# EVIL IN MEDIEVAL TIMES

Okay, this one's kind of a no-brainer. "Medieval" has the word "evil" right in it. They may not have spelled it the way we do, but they knew evil when they saw it.

### Royals

These people were downright cruel. They forced jesters to tell jokes all day long: that's no way to make a living. They would behead you for saying "Please" instead of "Thank you." And they married their own cousins. I mean, who does that?

## The Feudal System

This horrendous system forced people into a rigid class structure with no ability to transcend their social position or to ever rise out of poverty. Which probably made sense if you were big King Richy McWealthalot, but not for the hundred thousand other people. Evil!

## Famine

Not eating is bad. 'Nuff said.

## Dragons

These fire-breathing baddies could turn even the prettiest princess into toast. Wait, were those real or not? I saw them in a movie once, so I'm pretty sure they were real. And there was that one time I fought Parable the Dragonpus, so yeah, they're real.

# WHEN IN HISTORY WOULD YOU WANT TO GO?

If you could go back in time—and believe me, I'm working on an -inator that will let you do just that—where would you like to go? And when? Draw a picture of yourself in your favorite period from the past. Then make it evil!

# THE DOOFENSHMIRTZ WAY:
## WRITE A HISTORICAL CHAPTER WITHOUT DOING ANY RESEARCH

So let's pretend you're writing a book with a chapter that deals with history and you have no idea what really happened *last week*, let alone years and years ago. This is purely hypothetical and doesn't relate to me at all. Really.

Instead of doing research or "work," it's much easier to make stuff up. Here's how!

**A.** Make up the name of an evil person who was a big mover and shaker in the time period you are writing about. Make sure it is long and hard to pronounce so no one will question you. Like Hieronymus Schastikovistan. Sounds impressive, huh?

**B.** If you don't know exactly what took place back then, just end your sentences with phrases like "and whatnot" or "etcetera" or "and stuff like that." That makes it seem like you *know* there's more to the story, but you just can't be bothered to list it, and write it down, and whatnot.

**C.** Add one really specific detail that no one can possibly prove did or didn't happen. Did you know George Washington once carved the Capitol building into an apple? You see what I did? Could be true, could be false. Who can say?

**D.** Tie it all up with a strong summary that dares anyone to contradict you.

And that's exactly and precisely how you write a historical chapter without doing any research. So there.

# NOW **YOU** WRITE ABOUT SOMETHING YOU KNOW ABSOLUTELY NOTHING ABOUT!

**1.** Pick one of these random historical topics that you have never even heard of.

**The Fall of Rome • The Gold Rush • Perry's First Birthday**
**The French and Indian War • Doof's Wedding • The Moon Landing**

**2.** Don't do any research or even stop to think.

**3.** Start writing!

# WHO IN HISTORY WOULD YOU WANT TO MEET?

If you could go back in time (Seriously, I'm working on it. Back off, buddy!), who would you want to meet?

_____

If you could ask the person only THREE questions, what would you ask?

**1.** _____

_____

**2.** _____

_____

**3.** _____

_____

# INSPIRATION FOR THE EVIL SOUL: THE HISTORY EDITION

So you rolled out of bed this morning and you're just not feeling particularly evil today, huh? Believe you me, it's happened to the worst of us, including a certain someone named Genghis Khan. This was way back before he conquered half the world with his fearsome Mongol hordes.

• • • • • • • • • • • • • • • • • • • • • • •

At the time, Genghis was moping around, working the late-night drive-through shift at some Mongolian fast-food place, and his life was going nowhere. Well, one night, a woman drove an oxcart full of kids through his drive-through line. The kids were yelling and jumping and misbehaving and generally driving her nuts.

"Maybe they'll settle down when they're not so hungry," Genghis offered as he handed them their greasy sacks of ancient Mongolian food. The woman sighed, not really believing him.

"If I ran the world," she wearily joked, "the first thing I'd do is outlaw errands."

As she drove away, Genghis laughed . . . and then it hit him. Rule the world! That's what he should do! Well, without another word, he took off his hat and apron, quit his job, and went out to fulfill his evil destiny!

So when you're feeling less than evil, get up off your behind and start making someone's life miserable! You can do it!

# DRAW DOOF!

I couldn't finish the chapter without giving you a chance to create your own artistic impression of the most influential evil person in history . . . me!

# CHAPTER 3:
# EVIL FROM A TO Z

Everything you always wanted to know about evil, but were afraid to ask: A list of everyday things and why they are actually evil. (Like bunnies. Don't get me started!)

## Aardvarks

What is the deal with this guy? Just who does he think he is? He's SOOO important, he has to have *two* A's at the beginning of his name to make sure he's at the top of the list and the first one to get called on in class. If you ask me, I think he has an inferiority complex because he's just the poor man's anteater. He's not even that evil and certainly doesn't deserve to be first on this list, but there he is! Ugh, it's so infuriating.

## Almond Brittle Bits

Okay, first, let me say, I looooove almond brittle. Love it! But you know those little bits of almond brittle that get stuck between your teeth? I hate those. They take the pristine beauty of almond brittle and ruin it. Then you spend the rest of the night pushing at them with your tongue while searching for an all-night toothpick dispensary. Evil!

## Blimps

Every time I've used a blimp (which is more often than you might think), it pops. Or worse, it springs a leak and does that cartoony thing where it zigzags back and forth through the sky like a clown's balloon at a kiddie party. It's a cruel, vindictive conveyance, period.

## Bunnies

Oh, sure, they may look cute with their downy fur and wriggling little noses, but these long-eared pests are tools of the underworld, bent on world domination and complete control of Earth's carrot supply.

## Child TV Stars

What lamebrained TV executive looked at these kids and said, "Yeah. Let's put these yapping monkeys on the screen twenty-four hours a day with their annoying catchphrases and incessant mugging for the camera, driving our viewers away in droves. That's a good idea!" Evil!

### Daughters

Okay, maybe they don't turn out as wicked as you had hoped, but you can always dream, can't you?

### Drive-through Attendants

You know when you go to a fast-food restaurant and you use the drive-through window because you think it will save time, but then some Neanderthal can't seem to understand a single thing you say and you end up paying twenty bucks for someone else's order? Now tell me *that's* not evil.

### Entitled Drivers

Who are these self-important jerks in their pricey German cars who think they own the road? You know what they own? My eternal wrath!

**Figgy Pudding**

Disgusting! I don't even know why I have the stuff in my fridge to begin with. I'm sure it would take the same amount of time and money to make something tasty like chocolate pudding, or even vanilla, but noooo, someone had to get all creative and muck it up.

**Flying Skiff**

Have I ever taken this out and NOT crashed?!?

## Hot Dogs

Why would anyone eat this iffy combination of pig toes and sawdust when they could have a Doofenshmirtz Quality Bratwurst? I'll tell you why—because they are evilly delicious.

## Lawn Gnomes

C'mon, just look at them! Even without my emotionally scarring personal backstory revolving around one of them, you can just look into their eyes and see they are up to no good.

## L.O.V.E.M.U.F.F.I.N.

I am a proud (well, maybe "proud" is selling it a little too hard)
member of L.O.V.E.M.U.F.F.I.N., the League Of Villainous
Evildoers Maniacally United For Frightening Investments in
Naughtiness. It says it right there in the title. We're evildoers.
Doing evil. Now if you asked me for a list of the evil things
we've actually *accomplished*, that's another thing.

## My Couch

It's an eyesore. And I think there's something living in the
cushions. What's that about?

## O.W.C.A.

Okay, I realize that the Organization Without a Cool
Acronym actually FIGHTS evil, so it's weird that
they are on this list, but have you seen their
dental plan? It's not even a plan; it's just a guy
named Steve with some floss
and a pair of pliers. Thank
you, but no thank you.

## Pigeons

These rats with wings may SEEM innocent enough, ready to be zapped with a Poop-inator to ruin your brother's ceremony, but they don't care who they defile and they'll turn on you, buddy, mark my words!

## Plastic Packaging

Have you ever gone to the Googolplex Mall or, ooh, one of those big-box stores like the Superduper Mega Superstore that sells everything from hamster food to whitewall tires? And you buy, like, a little, tiny thing of toner for your printer for, like, ninety-five bucks? (Note to self: add "toner" to evil list.) And the itty-bitty toner is encased in enough plastic to mummify a grown man. And then you can't get it off without scissors, a butcher knife, and a flamethrower. That's evil with a capital E.

## Platypus

I have no idea why this is on the list. I don't have any feelings one way or another about a cute little platypus.

## Platypus, Perry the

Evil! Okay, to be honest, this one's a little confusing because he's not evil in GENERAL, in fact he's quite the opposite, but he is very cruel toward ME. Trust me, anyone who hits me repeatedly with his beaver tail on a daily basis is being cruel.

## Pretendy the Practice-pus

This little guy is a stand-in I made for Perry the Platypus so I could, you know, practice trapping him and rehearse my backstories and stuff. You get the idea. But the evil part of this seemingly innocuous hunk of wood is that he makes it seem so EASY to defeat him. I beat Pretendy the Practice-pus, like, nine times out of ten, and then when Perry the Platypus shows up: BOOM! It's like a whole different ball game. That's just not cool, dude.

## Robots

Robots are not inherently good or evil but can be programmed to be whatever you want. Or at least that's the common perception. When it comes to Norm, however, I've done all I can to crank his evil setting up to eleven, but he still walks around with that dumb smile on his face wanting to play catch. Although there was that one time I was stuck doing jury duty and Norm took the initiative and nearly destroyed all of Danville, so I guess I have to give him props for that.

## Sarcastic Norm Head

This guy is more obnoxious than evil, but he insisted that I put him on the list and wouldn't shut up until I did. Like I said, obnoxious!

## Self-destruct Buttons

Hey, I wouldn't use them if they weren't evil. Out of all the buttons, this one's the most evil of them all.

## Used-car Dealers

I took in my '75 station wagon and the guy gave me three hundred bucks for it. Three hundred bucks?!?! I had more than three hundred bucks' worth of change left between the seats! Anyway, I go past the place the next day and the same guy is selling it for twenty-five hundred! Evil!

## Zzyzx

It's the name of a real town, I swear, and a great word to use in a game of Hangman, but come on! Any place named Zzyzx has to be villainous, right?

WELCOME TO
ZZYZX

# CHAPTER 4:
# EVIL AND YOU

Okay, picture me holding my hands out. In one hand I have evil and in the other hand I have you. Now imagine me clapping my hands together. That's what this chapter is about.

(No, it's not about clapping. It's about bringing you and evil together. I thought that was obvious.)

# HOW EVIL ARE YOU?

Now that you've read a few chapters about evil, let's find out about the evil in you! Choose the answer that best matches *your* experience.

**1) Most people who drop by my place are looking for:**

    A) Conversation

    B) A fight

    C) Evidence of my latest evil scheme

**2) If a friend needs someone to talk to, I usually:**

    A) Sit down and listen  B) Hide  C) Laugh at them

**3) I spend most of my free time**

    A) Doing good deeds

    B) Doing things that make me happy

    C) Building -inators to take over the Tri-State Area

**4) If my brother were being given an award, I would:**

    A) Definitely be there to cheer him on

    B) Send a nice note

    C) Concoct a scheme to humiliate him once and for all

**5) The person I spend the most time with is a:**

    A) Nemesis

    B) Enemy

    C) Platypus

**6) My decorating style could best be described as:**

    A) Bright and sunny

    B) Dark and moody

    C) Evil villain's lair, circa 1983

## SCORING:

Give yourself one point for each time you answered A, two points for each B, and three points for each C, then add up your score. If you scored:

**6–9:** You call that evil? You wouldn't hurt a fly.

**10–14:** Congratulations! You're well on your way to becoming evil!

**15–18:** Whoa. Slow down there, kid. You're starting to scare even me.

# SEVEN HABITS OF HIGHLY EVIL PEOPLE

So you're on your way to a life of evil. Good. But how do you truly succeed in this new world of villainy? By hard work, dedication, and risk taking? No! Don't be ridiculous.

You succeed by stealing ideas from the successfully malicious people who came before you. At least, that's what every evil person I know does. (And 97.2% of those that I don't know.*) Follow their effective habits and you will soon be just as successful. Possibly.

*Results may vary.

1) Each morning when you get out of bed, give thanks for the problems you are about to cause other people.

2) Cross your fingers every time you make a promise.

3) Never floss.

4) Start evil rumors about yourself that are completely untrue.

5) Before you act, think carefully about all your options, then pick the worst one possible.

6) When in doubt, lie. Lie like the wind!

7) If you can't think of anything nice to say, say it louder.

# HOW TO RECOGNIZE EVIL PEOPLE

When you turn villainous, you join a unique group of people. There are lots of us out there (especially at bus terminals and bingo halls), but you have to know how to recognize us if you want to join our ranks.

Evil People **Don't**: Shop for perfume and doilies.

Evil People **Do**: Shop for traps and cages.

Evil People **Don't**: Offer to take pictures of other people.

Evil People **Do**: Jump into the background to ruin pictures of other people.

Evil People **Don't**: Flip their naturally curly hair and giggle.

Evil People **Do**: Twirl their menacing mustaches and cackle. (Especially if they're girls.)

Evil People **Don't**: Collect stuffed animals.

Evil People **Do**: Collect real animals that have been stuffed.

# NOW TO RECOGNIZE EVIL PEOPLE

Now we see if you were actually paying attention. Ha! Take a close look at the "gentlemen" in the two images below and see if you can tell which one is evil.

**ANSWER:** The one on the left is clearly thinking sinister thoughts, while the guy on the right is imagining a field of lollipops and daisies or something. What's his deal anyway?

## EVIL IN DANVILLE

One of the best places to look for evil is right in your own backyard. Well, not literally your "backyard." That would be dumb. I mean your neighborhood. Or in this case, my neighborhood, Danville!

• • • • • • • • • • • • • • • • • • • • • • • • • • • •

# L.O.V.E.M.U.F.F.I.N.

The League Of Villainous Evildoers Maniacally United For Frightening Investments in Naughtiness is an organization of the worst of the worst. Or at least the worst of the worst within easy driving distance of Danville. Together we give the animal agents of O.W.C.A. a run for their money. If they carry money. We meet two or three times a year at events that often feature copious amounts of potato salad. Members include me, Rodney, Dr. Diminutive, Dr. Bloodpudding, and that guy with the bad comb-over.

# RODNEY

*(formerly known as Aloyse Everheart Elizabeth Otto . . . oh, you know the rest.)*

A fellow L.O.V.E.M.U.F.F.I.N. scientist who thinks he's all that and a bag of chips. But other than building a giant fan and a girl robot, what has he really done? Nada. Zip. Zilch. The big goose egg. And does he even HAVE a nemesis trying to stop him? Doubtful. If so, I've never met him.

# DR. DIMINUTIVE

Another L.O.V.E.M.U.F.F.I.N. baddie, this guy is shortsighted, short-tempered, and, well, short. It's right there in his name, so no one should be surprised that he's vertically challenged. I think he fights a yak or a gnu or something vaguely cowlike, but I can't be sure.

# VANESSA DOOFENSHMIRTZ

This well-dressed diva of evil is the pinnacle of evilosity, feared and respected in the community of evil. She is so evil that—uh—

Okay, she's not really evil, but a father can dream, can't he?

She does show promising signs that she might someday TURN evil though.

1) She wears all black.
2) She has an attitude (especially with me!).
3) She likes punk. Or goth. Or Visigoths.
   One of those things.

# ARE YOU TRULY EVIL?

Okay, I'm going to paint a picture for you. No, not a literal picture; that would be too nice. It's a mental picture, an imagined situation, and you have to write down how YOU would react in that situation.

Picture yourself as a brilliant, maniacal evil scientist, boyishly handsome even if SOME people say your nose is too long.

You have concocted a convoluted scheme to take over the Tri-State Area with your new Lighter-than-air-inator! (To clarify, it makes other things lighter than air. The -inator itself is ridiculously heavy.)

Suddenly, an obnoxious little platypus agent bursts in, uninvited, with a clear agenda to ruin all your hard work.

You have your -inator, a trap made of cream cheese, and a pocket full of those little twist-tie things that they put on the end of the bags that sliced bread comes in—you know what I'm talking about. Anyway, it's you against the platypus.

NOW—what do you do next?! On the next page, write out exactly what you would do to thwart your opponent.

ONCE UPON A TIME, IN MY HOME COUNTRY OF DRUSSELSTEIN...

...AN EXTREMELY HANDSOME YOUNG MAN WAS WORKING THE FIELDS, HERDING RABBITS.

THE YOUNG MAN WAS PAID FOR HIS EFFORTS WITH THE PICK OF THE LITTER.

IT WOULDN'T FIT IN HIS POCKETS...

...SO HE SET IT DOWN JUST FOR A SECOND TO DO SOMETHING DUMB. AND OF COURSE, IT RAN AWAY.

THE MORAL? "A FOOL AND HIS BUNNY ARE SOON PARTED."

WAIT A SECOND, I JUST REALIZED I'M THE FOOL IN THIS SCENARIO!

CURSE YOU, CRUEL MORAL!!

OOF!

CURSE YOU, *PERRY THE PLATYPUS!*

NORM, A LITTLE HELP HERE.

SURE! IF YOU PROMISE.

NOT NOW, NC WE CAN TALK A THAT LATEN

BUT "LATER" *NEVER* COMES.

PLEASE, NORM, I'M *SLIPPING!*

I'VE GOT ALL THE TIME IN THE WORLD!

OKAY! OKAY! I PROMISE! *I PROMISE!*

UPSY-DAISY!

*ATER THAT NIGHT...*

WELL, I'M BUSHED. I'LL SEE YOU TOMORROW.

OH, NO. YOU *PROMISED.*

GOOD GRIEF. OH, ALL RIGHT.

SIGH!

"ONCE UPON A TIME, THERE WAS A LITTLE ROBOT WHO LOVED BUNNIES..."

BEDTIME STORIES

THE END!

# "NIGHT OF THE GOOZIM"

YOU KNOW, NORM, I'VE BEEN THINKING.

SOUNDS PAINFUL.

I'VE BEEN WASTING MY TIME TRYING TO *THINK UP* DESTRUCTIVE IDEAS, THEN *CREATE* DESTRUCTIVE -INATORS, AND THEN *ENACT* DESTRUCTIVE SCHEMES, WHEN DESTRUCTIVE THINGS *ALREADY* EXIST IN THE WORLD!

Coming Up: Danville's Next Average Model

LIKE THE *GOOZIM!*

IT'S JUST SITTING BACK IN DRUSSELSTEIN WAITING TERRIFY INNOCENT PEOPLE.. NOT-SO-INNOCENT PLATYF

ISN'T IT "PLATYPUSES"?

ALL I WILL HAVE TO DO IS FLY HALFWAY AROUND THE WORLD...

...TREK THROUGH UNCHARTED WILDERNESS TO HUNT DOWN THE EXTREMELY DANGEROUS CREATURE...

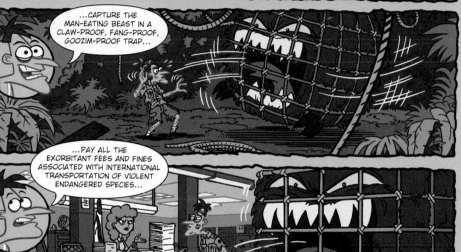

...CAPTURE THE MAN-EATING BEAST IN A CLAW-PROOF, FANG-PROOF, GOOZIM-PROOF TRAP...

...PAY ALL THE EXORBITANT FEES AND FINES ASSOCIATED WITH INTERNATIONAL TRANSPORTATION OF VIOLENT ENDANGERED SPECIES...

...AND THAT'S ASSUMING NOTHING GOES WRONG. BUT I'M PRETTY SURE SOMETHING WILL GO WRONG.

LATER...

HUH! NOTHING WENT WRONG. HOW ANTICLIMACTIC.

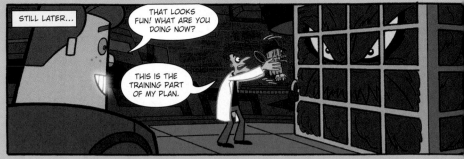

STILL LATER...

THAT LOOKS FUN! WHAT ARE YOU DOING NOW?

THIS IS THE TRAINING PART OF MY PLAN.

YOU REMEMBER PRETENDY THE PRACTICE-PUS, RIGHT?

WELL, BY TAUNTING THE GOOZIM MERCILESSLY WITH THIS STAND-IN, I AM TEACHING THE FUR-BRAIN TO LOATHE ANYTHING THAT LOOKS LIKE THIS FIGURE.

LIKE A TEAL LOAF OF BREAD!

WHAT?!? WELL, YES, I SUPPOSE, BUT I WAS THINKING MORE OF...

...PERRY THE PLATYPUS!

SLASH!

YIKES. THIS IS CRAZY SERIOUS.

ER THAT DAY...

AH, PERRY THE PLATYPUS! NO TRAP TODAY, JUST...THIS!

GRRRRR!

WHAT'S THE ER? GOOZIM GOT UR TONGUE?

NO FAIR! YOU'RE SUPPOSED TO GO *IN* THE GOOZIM, NOT *OVER* THE GOOZIM.

SWOOSH

HEY, KEEP YOUR WEBBY LITTLE APPENDAGES OFF OF MY THINGS!

GRRRRR!

WAIT! WHAT ARE YOU...?

UH-OH. YOU DON'T HAVE TO BE AN EVIL GENIUS TO SEE THAT THIS WON'T BE ENDING WELL.

CURSE YOU, PERRY THE PLATYPUUUUUUS, AND ALSO PRETENDY THE PRACTICE-PUUUUUUS!

THE E...

# THE POWER OF NEGATIVE THINKING

A great evil pioneer once said, "Happy thoughts do not an evil person make." And that great evil pioneer was ME!

It's all about the power of negative thinking. You have to rid yourself of those uplifting, optimistic thoughts and fill your head with seeds of negativity. To put it more simply, you need to be a Negative Neddy, not a Positive Polly. Here are some examples:

**You get half of a glass of water.**

Positive Polly sees it as half full.

Negative Neddy sees it as half empty. And no ice. And is that a lipstick stain on the rim? Did anybody even wash this glass? Ooh, it's payback time!

**It starts to rain.**

Positive Polly sees the silver lining and looks forward to the promise of a beautiful rainbow.

Negative Neddy sees all the cancelled ball games, soggy picnics, and ruined hairdos.

**A lost puppy is discovered on the street.**

Positive Polly cares for it, puts up posters all over town to find its owner, and, if no one claims it, she loves that puppy as the newest member of her family forever and ever.

Negative Neddy tells the dog that its chances of finding its family are slim to none and sends it off, sad and alone, never to wag its tail again.

Are **YOU** a Negative Neddy? Keep frowning!

# WHAT'S MY EVIL TALENT?

Each of us excels in different areas, and that holds true for evil talents, too. Now, you could spend months of trial and error, exploring all of the different skills to find out what you're good at . . . OR you can spin this WHEEL O' EVIL!

Cut out the wheel and punch a hole in the middle. Attach it with a brass pin to the next page and spin, spin, spin! Then go out immediately and buy another copy of this fine book, because you just ruined this one. Wait, definitely don't do anything I just mentioned.

# MAKE YOURSELF LOOK EVIL

Okay, this is the fun part. The rest of the book, pff! Forget it. This is where you get to make yourself look evil. Or "more evil" for those of you who already look iffy.

On this page draw a picture of how you look normally. Or if you really want to get fancy, copy or print a photo of yourself and paste it in the book.

Now, on this page, draw yourself again (or paste a copy of your picture again, fancy pants!), but this time make yourself really **EVIL**-looking.

Add horns, an evil mustache, creepy eyebrows, fangs, bolts in your neck. Go nuts!

**If you're going to be EVIL, you need to look EVIL!**

# VISIT EVIL PLACES

Even a foul family of atrocious adults and beastly children needs a little rest and relaxation from the hard work of being wicked. But when you book a trip for you and your not-so-loved ones, there's no reason it can't be inspirational as well as vacational. (Is that a word?) Avoid the crowded tourist destinations and boring natural wonders and seek out the truly heinous places around the world and you'll come home renewed and revitalized in new and nefarious ways.

## THE TOP TEN VILLAINOUS VACATION SPOTS FOR YOU AND YOUR EVIL FAMILY

### 10. BADBEARD LAKE

Featuring Spleen Island! This most hideous of places is believed to be haunted by the ghost of Badbeard the pirate, covered in hallucinogenic moss, sheltering a hideous sea hag, and hiding a cursed treasure and the bones of all those who have looked for it. Talk about getting your money's worth!

### 9. LAKE NOSE

Legendary home of the legend known as the Lake Nose Monster . . . allegedly.

## 8. THE OLD ABANDONED AMUSEMENT PARK

Step right up!
Now featuring tetanus!

## 7. TRANSYLVANIA

Vampires. Werewolves.
Mountainous castles of
doom. Need I say more?

## 6. TIBET

Not only does that abominable
snowguy live here, but also
Klimpaloon, the magical, old-
timey bathing suit that lives in
the Himalayas.

## 5. OMAHA, NEBRASKA

Let's just say that I had a bad experience there in the '80s and
leave it at that.

## 4. DOOFANIA

Okay, technically it doesn't exist anymore, but for those few precious hours when it DID exist, this place ROCKED!

## 3. THE SMILE AWAY REFORMATORY SCHOOL

Don't worry. The place looks nothing like it does in the brochure. I'm talking towering gray walls, guard towers with searchlights, and vicious guard dogs. Activities include breaking rocks, cleaning bathroom floors with a toothbrush, and mandatory buzz cuts! Let your imagination and enthusiasm drain away as they are forcibly replaced by structure, order, and total conformity!

## 2. DRUSSELSTEIN

It's like stepping back in time when you visit this backward land of yore. Stroll through the Doonkleberry fields or the Goozim Forest. Stop for a bite at Gunther Goat Cheese's or snap a pic of Princess Baldegunde's castle. But beware of the Kinderlumper!

# AND THE NUMBER ONE MOST VILLAINOUS VACATION SPOT FOR YOU AND YOUR EVIL FAMILY IS . . .

### Danville!

I know what you're saying. "No fair! He chose his own city! It's a blatant attempt to increase tourism!" And my response is, "Quiet down! This is my book, not yours." Besides, Danville is a veritable cornucopia of evilosity.

First of all, I'm here. That should be enough in itself. Secondly, Doofenshmirtz Evil Incorporated *and* L.O.V.E.M.U.F.F.I.N. are centered here. Thirdly, nearly half of all weird and unexplained creature sightings occur within city limits. I'm talking about Potato Gremlins, whalemingos, giant ants, Were-Cows, and even giant floating baby heads.

# GUIDE TO WRITING EVIL DEMANDS

At some time in every nefarious person's life, you're gonna have to write a list of your demands. How else will anyone know what you want? So why not make it fun? Use the multiple choice form below to create an instant statement of your demands that no one can refuse! (Hopefully.)

**TO** A) The Mayor B) Whom It May Concern C) Tony's Pizzeria,

**in case you haven't noticed, i have** A) filled your town with gelatin B) moved city hall to the moon C) two mismatched socks on.

**if you ever want things to return to normal, you must agree to my demands** A) immediately B) precisely C) with a positive attitude: no grumbling or whining or I won't accept it.

**on to the demands! First and Foremost i want** A) recognition of my brilliance with a statue in the town square B) ten million dollars C) a nice cup of chicken broth; I've been a bit under the weather lately.

**Secondly, i will need a luxurious getaway vehicle, preferably** A) a helicopter B) a Formula One race car C) anything other than a blimp. Seriously, floating with the wind is not gonna work here.

**Finally, and i know this is petty, but work with me on this one: For my own personal comfort, upon the receipt of my demands, i would like** A) a basket of fresh fruit waiting for me B) the soothing sounds of light jazz as I depart C) not to encounter any animals in fedoras during the proceedings.

**These are my demands. You have until** A) sunset B) noon tomorrow C) oh, let's say Arbor Day.

**If you have not met my demands by that time, i guarantee you that** A) you'll regret it B) I'll regret it C) I will start seriously considering a new line of work.

A) Sincerely yours,
B) Threateningly,
C) Love and kisses,

_____ (YOUR NAME HERE)

# INSPIRATION FOR THE EVIL SOUL

Not feeling evil enough yet? Don't worry. Not everyone can be an abomination right out of the gate. Maybe this story will boost your flagging spirits.

Once upon a time, there was a young boy named Victor. (I know saying "once upon a time" makes it feel like it's not true, but believe me, this one is as real as my Aunt Gunthoven's halitosis.)

Victor was a studious student who studied. A lot. He liked math and engineering and science, particularly biology, and was good at them. But no one recognized his brilliance. Not his teachers. Not his family. Not even the strange old woman who slept in the cafeteria.

So what did Victor do? Did he let others bring him down? Did he give up?

No!

He cobbled together a figure out of spare parts and lightning bolts and became Victor Von Frankenstein, the most famous mad scientist in the world!

In your face, schoolyard jerks!

So let that be a lesson to you. When the world is getting you down, you can always turn to evil!

# HOW TO MAKE AN EVIL WARNING SIGN

Now that you are on your way to being a truly malevolent bad guy, you should really warn those around you to keep out of your way. A clearly written sign on your door is a good first step.

Start by scrawling "KEEP OUT" in huge red letters across the top. Then sprinkle in any of the following phrases to help personalize your warning.

EVIL AFOOT!

This Means You!

YOU'VE BEEN WARNED!

You wouldn't like me when I'm ANGRY.

EVIL SCIENTISTS ONLY

VIOLATORS WILL BE IRRITATED

# CHAPTER 5: REFINING YOUR VILLAINOUS PERSONA

In the world of evil, it's all about perception. What people think of you is more important than what you actually are. (It's also true in entertainment, but that goes without saying.)

But this is actually a good thing for you beginners. It's much easier to LOOK evil than to do all the dirty work to actually BE evil . . . especially if you read this amazingly brilliant chapter by yours truly.

# YOUR EVIL LOOK DOS AND DON'TS

To be a sinister success, you need to look the part, as these critical DOs and DON'Ts clearly reveal.

**DO** apply big, bushy eyebrows to emphasize your angry brow. These can be weaved in or glued, but not stapled. (I learned that one from experience.)

**DO** maintain a sour expression. Most people look at your face first, and they had better see a frown. It's just a smile turned upside down!

**DO** turn up the collar on your cape. It lets people know you mean business. Oh, and wear a cape.

**DO** hunch over as if sneaking around. Good posture doesn't creep anyone out. (I'm lucky, as hunching comes naturally to me. It's a gift.)

**DON'T** top off your look with a silly hat. I know it's tempting, believe me, but you are trying to look maniacal, not like the life of the party.

**DON'T** wear plaid. Plaid says goofy and safe, not vicious and malicious.

**DON'T** wear sneakers. Nothing says amateur like a guy wearing old tennis shoes.

**DON'T** sport oversized belt buckles shaped like your favorite state. It's only cruel to people who appreciate fashion.

# YOUR EVIL LOGO

You may not have given a lot of thought to a logo, but it represents you and what you stand for. It goes on your building, your letters, maybe T-shirts, coffee mugs, decorative throw pillows, collectible spoons, and, eventually, when you take over your city or state, it will go on the new flag. You may have thousands of people saluting it against their wills every day for the rest of your life, so you don't want it to look lame, do you?

My logo includes the letters DEI. It stands for my company, Doofenshmirtz Evil Incorporated. Now, I don't know if you are incorporated or not. I did it for tax reasons primarily. If you don't have a company, you could use your own initials, I suppose, but put them in a creepy font that's intimidating. Maybe add a bat or something.

Here's another example: the O.W.C.A. logo. It's not evil at all. Not even a little bit. Tell you what, look at it and then try to do the exact opposite.

Now it's your turn to design your own logo on the next page . . . perhaps one with a monkey???

# Doofenshmirtz
## evil incorporated

## HAR D HAR
# TOY STORE

# THE DOOFENSHMIRTZ WAY: SOUNDING EVIL

When you scream something in anger off your balcony, you want it to be memorable, right? So here's how to piece together your own evil catchphrase! Pick one word or phrase from each column, put them together in the space below, and voilà! That's the memorable catchphrase that will define you to the world for all eternity.

| Curse | you | Perry the Platypus! |
| Forget | the world | lady! |
| A pox upon | humanity | Your Highness! |
| I am very aggrieved by | everyone but me | jerky! |
| Fiddlesticks to | my enemies | insignificant peon! |
| I wish the worst for | your momma | crab salad lover! |

_____    _____ ,   _____

# INSPIRATION FOR THE EVIL SOUL

My look wasn't always so refined and dapper. Yes, even I, Dr. Heinz Doofenshmirtz, have had periods where I didn't project the image of a successful, brilliant scientist. Let the following candid snapshots of my life be an inspiration to you. If I once looked this bad, maybe even YOU have a chance.

I looked funky . . . but not in a good way.

Sometimes looking "out of this world" is not a compliment.

I wish I could make this "look" disappear.

Oddly enough, I think it's the cape that ruins this look. (And I'm such a huge proponent of capes.)

No comment.

# DESIGN YOUR HIDEOUT

If a man's home is his castle, then a man's lair is his moat. . . or something like that. I'm not good with metaphors. Anyhoo, the lair is important because it's where you do all your nefarious planning and scheming. It needs to be suitably sinister, but also practical. I mean, spiderwebs may look creepy, but run into one of them while carrying your invention and you'll spend the rest of the day cleaning up broken -inator parts.

As you design your lair, choose the components that best suit you and your evil plans.

- Gargoyles
- Built-in traps
- A retractable roof
- A chair (very useful!)
- Good feng shui
- A front door (also very useful!)
- Rustic charm
- Secret passages
- A smoothie bar

The next page is all yours.
Start drawing your evil lair!!!

# PLAN YOUR OWN SCHEME

I know when you have a teacher like me, whom you admire and perhaps even adore, there is a tendency to do everything the way that he does it. And who can blame you? But it's important that you develop your own style, your own way of doing things. That's what will make you an original rather than a pale carbon copy. (Carbon copies are something we had back in Gimmelshtump instead of copy machines.) So I'm going to tell you about a scheme that I did, and then you figure out how you would do it in your own way. Coolio?

## THE GOAL:

To scare everyone out of city hall so I can march in and take over.

## THE -INATOR:

The Attacking-vending-machine-inator!

## THE SCHEME:

To enact this scheme, I will use everyone's innate fear of vending machines. You know, vending machines; those machines where you have to pump in eight or nine quarters to get one lousy sack of peanuts? And you know how you're always scared that someday they will rise up and take over the world? Me too. It's terrifying.

Well, with my Attacking-vending-machine-inator, I'll turn those rusty old appliances into *rampaging* old appliances, smashing through walls and shooting soda cans at the fleeing secretaries and bigwigs as they spill old, sticky candy bars in their wake. It's genius!

That's how I would do it. Now you try.

. . . . . . . . . . . . . . . . . . . . . . . . . . . . . . . . . . . . . . . . . . .

## THE GOAL:

To scare everyone out of city hall so you can march in and take over.

## THE -INATOR:

_____

## THE SCHEME:

_____

_____

_____

_____

_____

_____

_____

_____

_____

# FINISH THIS COMIC

So you think you're evil enough? Now it's time to put your money where your mouth is. And by "money" I mean "pencil," and by "mouth" I mean "this piece of paper." Draw yourself into these panels with me and add your own dialogue. Let's see if you can keep up with the master.

# WHICH EVIL CHARACTER ARE YOU MOST LIKE?

Now that you've really started to develop your own wicked persona, let's see what type of cruel character you are most like. Me? That jerk Rodney from L.O.V.E.M.U.F.F.I.N., who is always up in my grille? The infamous Dr. Jekyll/Mr. Hyde? Or that guy at the pizza place who always delivers my pizza cold? Let's find out!

**1. I hate all mankind, but what really bugs me is:**
   A) Rodney
   B) Doof
   C) Mirrors
   D) Customers who don't tip

**2. My favorite ice cream flavor is:**
   A) Doonkleberry
   B) Rodney Ripple
   C) Banana Split
   D) Pepperoni

**3. When I get angry:**
   A) I curse my nemesis.
   B) I don't get angry. I get even.
   C) I turn into a monster and then everything goes black.
   D) I purposely drop your pizza.

**4. I consider myself:**
A) An evil scientist
B) A scientist above all other scientists
C) A scientist first and a madman second
D) An actor. This is just my day job.

**5. My favorite game to play is:**
A) Poke the Goozim with a Stick
B) Taunt Doofie
C) Hyde and Seek
D) Toss the Pizza

## 6. My name sort of rhymes with:

A) Goof and Spurts
B) Cod Knee
C) Rock Her Heckle and Sister Fried
D) The Meatsa Fly

## SCORING

Give yourself one point for each time you answered A, two for each B, three for each C, and four for each D, and then total your score.

### 6–8 Points
Congratulations! You're just like me!

### 10–15 Points
What is your problem? One Rodney is already one Rodney too many!

### 16–20 Points
You are two-faced (literally) and a small step away from multiple personalities. Good job!

### 21–24 Points
You are a horrible pizza deliveryman and a horrible human. No tip for you!

# CHAPTER 6:
## THE ONE
# SECRET
## TO INSTANT
## EVIL SUCCESS

So you thought you could skip ahead, huh?

This is a fake-out chapter for anyone who turned straight to this page.

If I actually KNEW this, do you think I'd be wasting my time writing a book?

# CHAPTER 7:
# MY ARCH NEMESIS

You can learn loads of things by taking a look at one of the most challenging nemeses in the history of nemesosity: Perry the Platypus. Clearly, he was assigned to be MY nemesis because I am the most challenging evil scientist in the history of evil scientistery. Evil scientistness? Evil scientifica?! How should I know? I'm a scientist, not an English teacher!

# UNWANTED

## PERRY THE PLATYPUS

### UNWANTED FOR:
- Escaping traps
- Thwarting schemes
- Hitting evil scientists

### REWARD: $371.28

## FROM THE MOUTH OF AGENT P

The Top Ten Quotes from Perry the Platypus!

10) Dgdgdgdgdgdg

9) Dgdgdgdgdgdg

8) Dgdgdgdgdgdg

7) Dgdgdgdgdgdg

6) Dgdgdgdgdgdg

5) Dgdgdgdgdgdg

4) Dgdgdgdgdgdg

3) Dgdgdgdgdgdg

2) Dgdgdgdgdgdg

1) Dgdgdgdgdgdg

# TOP TEN MOST ANNOYING THINGS ABOUT PERRY THE PLATYPUS

Sure, he's a good listener and a loyal nemesis, but he's also a pain in the patootie. Here's how:

**10) He's prompt.**
You know the type. He is ALWAYS punctual, so anytime you're running a little bit late or don't quite have your trap ready, he shows up right on time to rub it in your face.

**9) He hits really hard.**
I mean, I know the whole fighting thing is a key part of being a nemesis, but, man, can't he pull a punch every now and then?

**8) That sound he makes.**
Seriously, what is that? A purr? A growl? A hairball? What?!

**7) His clothes.**
Have you noticed he never wears anything but a hat? Who does that? If I tried that, I'd be arrested!

**6) That look.**
You know that look he gives you when he thinks you're being dumb or rude or obvious or evil or inconsiderate or anything else? That look is annoying.

**5) He picks his teeth.**
Most people don't know this about him, but give that guy a toothpick and he goes to town, and thirty minutes later he's still pickin' away. No, wait, that's my cousin Sal. Never mind.

### 4) He's so secretive!

Okay, okay, I guess that shouldn't surprise me because the word "secret" is right there in his job description—"secret agent"—but c'mon! I've fought the guy for YEARS and I don't even know where he lives.

### 3) His breath.

Smells like chewed grubs.

### 2) His silence.

Yes, I know he's the strong, silent type, but he takes it too far. Do you have any idea how hard it is to keep up both ends of the conversation every day? It's like talking to a brick wall . . . a brick wall that hits you.

### And the Number One Most Annoying Thing About Perry the Platypus:

### 1) He leaves those wet, webbed footprints everywhere.

# DO YOU KNOW YOUR NEMESIS?

The best way to defeat your enemy is to know everything you can about him . . . or to use a huge -inator that zaps him to the moon, but let's stick with the first way. How well do you know Perry the Platypus?

1. Perry the Platypus works for O.W.C.A., which stands for: A) the One World Combat Agency B) the Organization Without a Cool Acronym C) the Olive Workers Combine Association D) Our Workforce Contains Animals

2. Perry the Platypus hides his secret weapons: A) in his tool belt B) in his jet pack C) in his hat D) in his condo

3. Where does Perry the Platypus live? Seriously, if you know, tell me. Help a brother out

**4.** He rarely uses it, but how does Perry the Platypus deliver poison? A) Barbs in his ankles B) Fangs in his bill C) Pincers in his tail D) Overnight express mail

**5.** The man who gives Perry the Platypus his orders is: A) Major Monty Monogram B) Major Francis Monogram C) Major Pain Monogram D) Carl

**6.** Perry the Platypus only tries to defeat me: A) when he feels like it B) when he's ordered to do it C) when I'm doing evil D) when the groundhog sees his shadow

**7.** When I trap Perry the Platypus, he usually listens politely to my scheme and then: A) escapes B) gently falls asleep C) growls angrily D) traps me!

**8.** If I had five apples, and I gave one apple to Perry the Platypus, I would: A) have four apples left B) still have five apples, because I'm gonna take that apple back as soon as he's trapped C) be much more generous than usual D) not advise him to bite the apple. It's probably a trap.

**9.** Perry the Platypus is a suave, semiaquatic personification of unstoppable dynamic fury, but what do most people think about platypuses? A) They are difficult pets. B) They are good with kids. C) They don't do much. D) They cause the flu.

**10.** If I was going to get a present for Perry the Platypus on his birthday—not that I'm going to, this is just a hypothetical question—what do you think he'd prefer? A) A gift card B) A new grappling hook C) His own entrance to my lair . . . like a doggie door, but for a platypus D) A nice cold cuts platter

**I'm Heinz Doofenshmirtz and I've Got All the Answers!**

To the quiz.

**ANSWERS:**
**1) B**, and they are so proud of it. **2) C**; that's the only place he CAN hide them. **3)** Even a general neighborhood would help. Please? **4) A.** Disgusting, isn't it? **5) B.** Although "C" is a funnier answer. **6) C.** He's very particular about that. **7) A.** This was an EASY one! Why are you even looking at the answer?! **8)** What? Oh, sorry, to be honest, I'm not really paying attention anymore. **9) C.** I wish! **10) A.** I think I'm going with the gift card. I know, I know, it's so impersonal, but at least I know he'll get something he actually wants.

# FILL IN FOR DOOFENSHMIRTZ!

Clearly, no one can fill in for me during my epic confrontations with Perry the Platypus, but here is your chance to try. Simply fill in the blanks in this blow-by-blow description of our last encounter.

It was a/an _____ day in Danville when Agent P
ADJECTIVE

_____ broke into Doofenshmirtz Evil Incorporated
ADVERB

and was quickly trapped in a/an _____.
NOUN

"Ah, Perry the Platypus," Dr. Doofenshmirtz said, "what an

un- _____ surprise. And by that I mean completely
ADJECTIVE

_____!"
SAME ADJECTIVE

Dr. Doofenshmirtz then unveiled his latest _____
ADJECTIVE

invention, the Morph-inator, designed to transform Perry into

a less _____ opponent. With a/an _____,
ADJECTIVE                                    SOUND EFFECT

Dr. Doofenshmirtz fired the -inator, instantly turning Perry into

a/an _____ _____.
ADJECTIVE          NOUN

continued on next page ⟶

"Well, that's not what I expected," Dr. Doofenshmirtz

said _____ as he rubbed his _____. "Maybe
        ADVERB                                    BODY PART

if I adjust the _____ . . ."
                  NOUN

But as Dr. Doofenshmirtz turned to his device, Perry

_____ escaped and began to _____ Dr.
   ADVERB                                        VERB

Doofenshmirtz in the stomach. Dr. Doofenshmirtz stumbled

back into his -inator with a/an _____ and it fired
                                 SOUND EFFECT

another _____ blast, hitting Dr. Doofenshmirtz square
          ADJECTIVE

in the _____. The _____ scientist rapidly
        BODY PART              ADJECTIVE

morphed into a mix between a/an _____ and
                                    NOUN

a/an _____.
        NOUN

"You think this will stop me, Perry the Whatever-You-Are?"

Dr. Doofenshmirtz howled as he grabbed a/an _____ and
                                              NOUN

hurled it at Agent P. But Perry was so _____ and
                                         ADJECTIVE

_____ in his new form that he _____ dodged
   ADJECTIVE                               ADVERB

the object and began to _____ Dr. Doofenshmirtz mercilessly
                          VERB

With Dr. Doofenshmirtz subdued, Perry grabbed a/an

_____ and used it to destroy the -inator. Instantly, the

NOUN

two _____ opponents turned back into their normal

ADJECTIVE

selves. And as Perry jumped off the balcony with his _____,

NOUN

Dr. Doofenshmirtz yelled, "Curse you, Perry the Platy-_____!"

NOUN

# THE END.

# THE DOOFENSHMIRTZ WAY: HOW TO FIGHT A PLATYPUS

Yes, you can try to trap your nemesis. You can try to trick your nemesis. But try as you might to avoid it, the time will come when you have to FIGHT your nemesis. And if your archrival just happens to be a platypus, then here's what you need to know.

## Protect Yourself

The best defense is a good offense, and a good offense is all about preparing yourself ahead of time. (Can you prepare yourself AFTER it starts?! No, I don't think so!) I like to put padding under my lab coat or even those little foam peanuts that spill all over the floor when you get a package in the mail. These help to protect your important parts . . . like your everything.

## Use Your Environment

The platypus is a wily adversary (that means he fights good), so unless you've got a dangerous -inator in your pocket, you'd bet be prepared to improvise. Look around. Is there anything nearby that you could throw, swing, kick, or topple toward your foe? How about hiding places? Anywhere you could di to get away from the repeated, unrelenting blows? Or is there an exit door nearby? If so consider this gem of advice: run away!

THIS IS A STORY FROM MY HOME COUNTRY OF DRUSSELSTEIN.

I CALL IT "THE BOY WHO CRIED SPITZENHOUND."

WHEN I WAS A YOUNG LAD, I WOULD CRY OUT EVERY TIME I SAW THE SPITZENHOUND COMING.

BUT NO ONE BELIEVED ME.

EVEN WHEN I WAS ATTACKED BY THE SPITZENHOUND, NO ONE BELIEVED ME.

EVEN WHEN I WAS COVERED IN HOUND SALIVA, NO ONE BELIEVED ME.

EVEN WHEN I HAD A SPITZENHOUND LATCHED TO MY HINDQUARTERS, NO ONE BELIEVED ME.

THE MORAL OF THE STORY?

DON'T LIVE IN DRUSSELSTEIN.

*THE END!*

OKAY, SO TODAY'S EVIL SCHEME REVOLVES AROUND MY LIFELONG HATRED OF HOLIDAY MARSHMALLOW TREATS.

BACKSTORY TIME!

AS A SMALL CHILD IN GIMMELSHTUMP, I WAS ATTACKED BY A--

WAIT! WHAT ARE YOU--?

NO, NO, NO. YOU CAN'T JUST GO STRAIGHT TO BLOWING UP THE -INATOR. YOU HAVE TO ATTACK ME FIRST.

I MEAN, SERIOUSLY, WHERE DO THEY GET THESE KIDS?

NOT TO MENTION YOU REALLY SKIPPED THE WHOLE "GETTING TRAPPED" PART, BUT I'M WILLING TO OVERLOOK THAT SINCE YOU'RE A NEWBIE AND ALL.

OKAY, WHERE WAS I? OH, RIGHT. LOCK YOU UP. EXPLAIN MY PLAN. BACKSTORY. BACKSTORY. -INATOR.

NOW GRAB ME BY THE COLLAR. PICK ME UP. YOU CAN DO IT.

AND THROW ME AS HARD AS YOU CAN AT THE -INATOR.

THAT'S IT!

YES!

NOW I SAY, "OH, NO! NOT THE SELF-DESTRUCT BUTTON."

OKAY, THAT'S IT. SHOW'S OVER. MAKE YOUR DRAMATIC EXIT ALREADY.

CURSE YOU, TRISTAN THE TRAINEE!

NICE KID, BUT HE'S NO PERRY THE PLATYPUS.

THE END!

# "THE SUBSTITUTE"

AH, PERRY THE PLATYPUS!

BEHOLD, MY UPSIDE-DOWN-CAKE-INATOR

YOU SEE, BACK IN GIMMELSHTUMP, I WAS ALWAYS TERRIFIED OF UPSIDE-DOWN FOODS. SO I--

OKAY, I'M NOT DR. DOOFENSHMIRTZ. BUT HE DIDN'T WANT TO MISS HIS APPOINTMENT WITH YOU, SO HE ASKED ME TO STAND IN.

HE'S VERY BUSY TODAY AND COULDN'T BE INTERRUPTED, SO...

HE CAN'T BE BOTHERED AND I CAN'T TELL YOU WHERE HE IS.

PRIVATE

SO I NEEDED A LITTLE "ME" TIME TO WATCH MY STORIES! IS THAT SO EVIL?!

PRIVATE

THE EN

# "THE COMIC HIJINKS OF NORM AND DOOF"

THERE! THE NORM UPGRADES ARE COMPLETE.

TIME TO CELEBRATE!

NO, TIME FOR A MASSAGE.

THAT'S WHY I ADDED A SHIATSU SETTING ON YOUR DIAL.

I ENJOY WORKING WITH MY HANDS!

AY, NORM, 'S NOT GET RIED AWAY.

AROUND AND OVER AND THROUGH THE BUNNY HOLE.

OW OW OW! WHAT ARE YOU DOING?!?

ALL DONE! WOULD YOU LIKE IT SALTED OR PLAIN?

UGH-- I FORGOT ABOUT THAT PRETZEL-MAKING SETTING.

THE END!

# "PERRY THE...OCTOPUS?"

AH, PERRY THE PLATYPUS! I'VE FINALLY FIGURED OUT WHY YOU KEEP THWARTING ME.

IT'S YOUR SKILLS AS A *PLATYPUS!*

YES, REALLY. DON'T GIVE ME THAT LOOK.

SO SAY GOOD-BYE TO YOUR EXCEPTIONAL PLATY-TALENTS.

BEHOLD! MY PLAT-TO-OCT-INATOR! TO CHANGE YOU FROM A FORMIDABLE *PLAT*YPUS...

...INTO A COWARDLY *OCT*OPUS!

ZZZZAP!

OW! NO! HEY!

NOW YOU'RE HITTING ME EIGHT TIMES AS FAST!

LATER... HOW DID...? DON'

THE

## Fight Dirty

Most fighting disciplines tell you to fight with honor or to obey some code about self-defense. That's crazy! You're trying to win, right? So the best time to hit a platypus is when his back is turned, or the light is in his eyes, or you've just covered him in sticky bubble gum.

## Don't Forget the Tail

I can't tell you how many times I was THIS CLOSE to defeating Perry the Platypus when out of nowhere— WHACK! This fifth limb comes flying around and knocks me down flat. It's not fair when you think about it. I only have two hands and two feet, but HE has two hands, two feet, AND a prehensile tail! So heed my advice: beware of the tail!

Whoops. Those aren't fight poses, they're dance moves. Never mind.

# FINDING PERRY

I have often thought that if only I could find out where Perry the Platypus lived, I could go there and defeat him. Don't ask me why it would be easier at his place when I clearly have the home-field advantage at my place. The point is, I don't know where he lives and it would help if I could find him. That's where you come in.

Look at the mysterious, convoluted puzzle below and try to find Perry.

P E R R Y P E R R Y

P E R R Y P E R R Y

P E R R Y P E R R Y

P E R R Y P E R R Y

P E R R Y P E R R Y

# CHAPTER 8: YOUR ARCH NEMESIS

Now you are finally ready to take on your own arch nemesis!
Unless you skipped ahead to this chapter. Then you are in for a
world of pain.

# HOW TO SELECT AN ARCH NEMESIS

Hopefully, you'll be spending a lot of time with the reptile, mammal, or industrious insect that becomes your nemesis, so you'll want to make sure the two of you are well suited for each other. And I have just the thing to do that. Behold! My Nemesis-compatibility-quiz-inator!

1. **An ideal evening with my nemesis would include:** A) dinner and a movie B) trapping, escaping, and thwarting C) building an -inator, powering up an -inator, and watching the -inator self-destruct D) taking over the ENTIRE TRI-STATE AREA!!!

2. **When not fighting over evil schemes, I expect my nemesis:** A) to keep tabs on me anyway . . . to make sure I'm okay B) to be my wingman on crazy escapades and adventures C) to stay out of my hair, dude D) to bring enough takeout food for two

3. **It is most important to me that my nemesis:** A) lives in my area B) shares my interests C) has a bus pass D) doesn't chew his fingernails. Disgusting!

4. **When my adversary comes to my lair, I prefer that he:** A) calls first B) sneaks up behind me C) crashes through the ceiling D) breaks down the door

**5. I like to fight opponents who:** A) are smaller than me
B) are semiaquatic C) eat flies D) don't speak

**6. I'm allergic to:** A) feathers B) fur C) long hair D) all of
the above

### Scoring
Give yourself one point for each A answer, two for each B, three for each C,
and four for each D. Then total your score.

### 1–8 Points
Your perfect nemesis is short, hairy, and loves long walks on the beach.
Expect a lot of crouching and stooping when you fight Agent W, the weasel.

### 9–14 Points
The adversary you would be most compatible with is brave, cunning, and
agile. But you're not taking Perry the Platypus, so you can forget about that
right now. Try Agent C, the chicken.

### 15–20 Points
Agent F, the frog. Your ultimate foe is a bulbous-eyed, swamp-dwelling
amphibian. I hope you're proud of yourself.

### 21–24 Points
You are perfectly suited for
a mindless powerhouse like
Agent R, the rhinoceros.
Expect to be pummeled to pulp.

# DESIGN A NEMESIS

In a perfect world, what would your true nemesis look like? Close your eyes, free your mind, and imagine your dream adversary. Is he big and brawny? Old and ornery? How should I know? It's in YOUR head!

Okay, now open your eyes and on the next page draw, draw like the wind!

# INSPIRATION FOR THE EVIL SOUL:
## STUCK WITH A NEMESIS

You probably look at Perry the Platypus and me and think it's a match made in heaven. But it wasn't always this way. Back in the day, O.W.C.A. assigned agents willy-nilly, with no regard for personality conflicts or basic compatibility issues . . . like a bad blind date!

Why, when I first met Perry the Platypus, I didn't even know what kind of an animal he was. Who's ever heard of a *teal* platypus?! And I gotta tell you, he got on my last nerve . . . always staring at me, judging me. You know how he is.

Well, I was ready to call it quits. I even called Major Monogram to see if I could get another nemesis assigned. Something a little less semiaquatic. But thank goodness, Francis said to give it a little more time to see if things could work themselves out. And you know what? They did!

Now I wouldn't trade my nemesis for anyone in the world. Oh, sure, he still infuriates me and I try to eliminate him on a daily basis, but that's just what I do.

So, if your first encounter with your mortal foe isn't perfect, don't despair! It gets better . . . usually.

# THE DOOFENSHMIRTZ WAY: HOW TO TRAP YOUR NEMESIS

If you ever expect to have a few quiet moments to explain your entire plan to your nemesis, you're going to need to trap him first. Trapping is an art form—maybe not up there with classical sculpture, but certainly better than knitting. So here are some top trap tips.

## STRENGTH—STRONG LASTS LONG

For some reason, steel, cement, and iron traps seem to last longer than, say, wicker. So when designing your trap, avoid materials like tissue, old rubber bands, and wet newspaper.

## RECYCLE—USE WHAT'S LYING AROUND THE LAIR

This is not only good for the environment, it's also good for your pocketbook. As an added bonus, it's easy to hide your trap in plain sight. Who would suspect that your pile of computer wires and cables is really a sinister trap?

## HOLES—TRICKIER THAN THEY SEEM

Your trap must have holes large enough so your prisoner can get air, but small enough that they can't escape. This is particularly a challenge with Agent S, the snail.

## BUTTONS—NOT IN YOUR BEST INTEREST

I know it goes against your instincts, but do NOT install any of these buttons: Quick-Release, Auto-Eject, etc. Believe me, I learned this the hard way.

# DESIGN YOUR OWN TRAP

Traps are an essential part of dealing with your nemesis. The most important objective of any trap is keeping your opponent confined long enough for you to explain your scheme AND your tragic backstory. But it's also nice if your trap fits with the overall theme of your scheme. I call it the scheme theme.

So let's say your scheme involved race cars. You plan to cheat in a race to win the prize money. In that case, a seat-belt trap might be fun. Ooh, or a stack of tires that falls over your nemesis and holds him down. Any trap that has something to do with the theme of cars or racing will show your enemy that you care enough to make that little extra effort.

On the next page, design a trap that no agent could possibly escape from. If it's really good, I might steal it for myself!

SLam!

125

# TOP TEN WAYS TO MOCK O.W.C.A. AGENTS

Playful banter and witty wordplay are essential parts of your interaction with your nemesis, and you'll want to be sure to cut him down emotionally before he beats you up physically.

1. Say: "Nice fedora. Do they make any that DON'T make you look lame?"

2. Just point and giggle. They hate that.

3. Try saying, "You're just mean. You're inhuman. Oh, that's right, you're NOT human. Ha!"

4. Ask if they're house-trained.

5. Say something like, "Nice conversation skills, buddy. I can see why you work alone!"

6. You could offer: "I'd ask you to join me for dinner, but I don't have any kibble!"

7. Or try: "What? No hypersonic lock pick in your fedora? I guess a cool acronym isn't the only thing you guys don't have."

8. With a mocking tone say: "Oh, look at me! I'm an animal secret agent and my name is based on the first letter of my species. How clever!"

**9.** Offer to take them for a walk.

**10.** You can always ask: "So, how are the hair balls lately?"

# WHAT TO DO IF YOU ARE THWARTED

This is a tough one, but believe you me, it's one you need to face head-on. This is a fact: you are going to get thwarted every day, day after day, until the day you succeed. That's just the way it goes. So accept it and use these tips to handle the inevitable thwarting.

## HOLD YOUR HEAD UP HIGH

Being thwarted is nothing to be ashamed of—unless you have two black eyes and the explosion that destroyed your -inator also blew your clothes off.

## LEARN FROM YOUR MISTAKES

If you did something really, really, really stupid, next time don't do that!

## TRY. TRY AGAIN

"He who doesn't try can't have Doonkleberry pie." That's an old Drusselstinian proverb.

## ADHESIVE BANDAGES AND PEROXIDE

You know that phrase "Pour salt in your wounds." DON'T DO THAT! That's crazy talk.

# CHAPTER 9: -INATORS AND YOU

Now that you have a nemesis, how do you defeat him?

Two words: -inator!

Oh, I guess that's only one word.

Actually, it's just part of a word.

Never mind.

# -INATORS THAT CHANGED THE WORLD!

It's not only men and women and a few ornery kids who have made our planet such a great breeding ground for evil. It's the -inators! Huge, volatile machines that explode more often than not, but that impact our lives more than you know.

## NAIL-POLISH-REMOVE-INATOR

Okay, this one may not have changed YOUR world, but for the working moms of the Tri-State Area, this time-saving device is a miracle worker that keeps them looking their best and feeling their best! Order yours today! (Patent Pending)

## CHANGE-THE-WORLD-INATOR

Yes, this one's pretty obvious for the category of "-Inators that Changed the World." Some might say TOO obvious. Some people will do anything to get themselves on a list.

## AMNESIA-INATOR

This was one of my most powerful -inators and I think it did something really monumental once, but for some reason I can't remember. Do you remember it, Perry the Platypus? Ah, you wouldn't tell me if you did.

## INDUSTRIAL-REVOLUTION-INATOR

I wish I could take credit for this one, but it was Alexander Industrial who came up with this doozy of a device. Almost overnight, it literally turned a dirty, sweaty, labor-driven world into a dirty, sweaty, machine-driven world. Kudos to youdos, Alex!

# WHY A SELF-DESTRUCT BUTTON?

Sometimes people ask me, "Why do you always install a self-destruct button?" You might as well ask, "Why is the sky blue?" (Answer: berry stains!)

Self-destruct buttons are as natural to -inators as the smell of trash is to New York City. A self-destruct button is a symbol of professionalism that lets the world know you mean business. A self-destruct button tells your nemesis you'd rather destroy your life's work than see it used for good.

# DESIGN YOUR OWN -INATOR

Boom! Let's see what you got. No lessons. No tips. Just hit the ground running and create your own diabolical -inator.

Okay, okay, I'll help a little. Here are a few "classic" features you may want to include.

- **Emergency backup power**
- **Glow-in-the-dark dials**
- **A 360-degree swivel base**
- **Smell-o-rama odor**
- **A self-destruct button**
- **A jet-powered fusion reactor**
- **A reverse button**
- **A coin-return slot**
- **A periscopic lens**
- **Turbines**
- **Lots of pointless blinking lights**

# -INATOR FILL-IN-THE-BLANKS STORY

Like building an -inator, this story takes the right parts in the right places to make a working device. Insert words in the instructions below or face my wrath!

A/An _____ man once said, "Building an -inator
ADJECTIVE

is like baking a/an _____." Clearly he was _____
NOUN                                        ADJECTIVE

and didn't know what he was talking about.

To build a/an _____ -inator, you must start with
ADJECTIVE

a/an _____ idea. For example, let's say you want to
ADJECTIVE

_____ the entire Tri-State Area by getting rid of all
VERB

the _____. Great! Now you are an evil _____
PLURAL NOUN                                         NOUN

with a purpose!

Next you'll need the raw materials to build your

_____ -inator, like _____, a big _____,
ADJECTIVE                        PLURAL NOUN              NOUN

and a self-destruct button. Oh, and it makes things _____
ADJECTIVE

if you have a spare _____ for a power source.
NOUN

_____ assemble your -inator in your _____
**ADVERB**                                              **ADJECTIVE**

lair. Now comes the fun part: naming your creation! You could

simply call it a/an _____-inator, but that's so _____.
                            **NOUN**                              **ADJECTIVE**

How about the _____-the-_____-inator? Or the
                            **VERB**                    **NOUN**

_____-_____-_____-inator?!
**ADJECTIVE**            **ADJECTIVE**          **NOUN**

You did it! _____, you made an -inator! Now,
                        **EXCLAMATION**

simply wait _____ for your nemesis to show up and
                    **ADVERB**

destroy it!

# GET TO THE "FIRE" BUTTON

Once you have built your -inator, it is ESSENTIAL that you get to the -inator and fire it before your nemesis can destroy it. This really should be obvious, but you'd be surprised how many times I've built an entire -inator and never got the chance to hit the "fire" button.

On the next page, help the handsome evil scientist reach the -inator before the pesky platypus agent can stop him. If you follow the right path, the line you draw will intersect a series of letters that spell out a particularly evil phrase. Go!

**FINISH**

# HOW TO MAKE AN -INATOR FROM NOTHING BUT A BROKEN WASHING MACHINE!

Okay, so you're probably asking yourself, "Why would I ever need to make an -inator out of a broken washing machine?" Well, smarty-pants, it's that kind of attitude that will get you in serious trouble when your nemesis has you cornered in a deserted Laundromat. So listen closely.

1. Take apart the washing machine with your screwdriver. Oh, yeah, I guess you'll need a screwdriver AND a broken washing machine.

2. Attach the motor to the base with six-inch bolts. Oh, and you'll need six-inch bolts. A broken washing machine, a screwdriver, and six-inch bolts.

3. Use the microcomputer in your phone to create a—oh, right. A broken washing machine, a screwdriver, six-inch bolts, a phone . . . probably some wire; better add in some basic circuitry and a perpetual power supply too while you're at it.

4. Now step back and enjoy your creation made from nothing but a broken washing machine!

# MEMORY QUIZ

A keen memory is vital to a successful evil villain. That one thing you forget may be the key to your thwarting! Well, the best way to improve your memory is to use it! Look at this picture of one of my -inators in action. Study it for sixty seconds, then turn the page and see how many questions you can answer about it.

**Memory Questions!**

1) What kitchen appliance is incorporated into the -inator?

2) Is the floor made of brick or wood?

3) How many -inator barrels (the pointy parts that shoot out laser blasts) can you see?

4) What am I doing with my hands?

5) Can you see the top of the -inator?

6) Can you see the bottom of the -inator?

7) Are my pants wrinkled? Seriously, because I don't want to have that happen again. How embarrassing.

8) There is a small white control panel near the bottom. Is it on the right or the left?

**Answers**

1) A hand mixer. You know, one of those things you use in the kitchen to mix things . . . by hand. 2) Wood. 3) Five. 4) They are clasped together. 5) No. 6) No. I guess this wasn't a very good picture to choose, was it? 7) No. 8) It's on the right. But it should be on "the wrong." Get it?